W9-AJQ-072

BROWNIES–THEY'RE MOVING!

by Gladys L. Adshead

pictures by Richard Lebenson

New York   Henry Z. Walck, Inc.

For Ann Lea from the
brownies and me with love

"Brownies—they're moving," shouted Biggest Brownie as he came skipping through the pine needles.

"Who's moving?" Middle-Size Brownie shouted back, cupping his mouth with his two hands.

"Old Grandmother and Old Grandfather," said Biggest Brownie. "I've run all the way to tell you."

He sat down, puffing and blowing, all out of breath, while the brownies gathered around him.

"What's moving?" asked Smallest Brownie.

"It means," Biggest Brownie explained, "they are going somewhere else to live."

All the brownies looked sad. They liked visiting Old Grandmother and Old Grandfather.

"How do you know?" asked Middle-Size Brownie.

"I've been listening to them talk," Biggest Brownie said. "You had better come quickly and listen."

The brownies lost no time. They went skippity-hop, skippity-hop as fast as they could, through the pine woods over the meadow to the little white house. Into the house they crept, but Old Grandmother

and Old Grandfather had finished their conversation.
Old Grandmother was washing the dishes. Old Grandfather was in the woodshed.

"Never mind," said Biggest Brownie, "this will
give us a chance to hide. Be very quiet."

"Underneath Old Grandmother's chair is a good place to hide," whispered Middle-Size Brownie in a very small voice.

Old Grandmother's back was turned and all the brownies crept under her chair without any difficulty at all.

"Will they talk again?" asked Smallest Brownie anxiously.

"Their old bones will get tired and they'll sit down again," Biggest Brownie replied. "Then we'll listen."

Old Grandmother finished drying the dishes. She was talking to herself. "Yes," she said, "this old house has too much work for old bones. Old Grandfather and I need a new LABORSAVING house."

She took a broom and swept the floor. The brownies were TERRIFIED that she would sweep under the chair—but she did not. She put her broom away, sighed, and sat down in her chair with a BUMP.

Smallest Brownie almost jumped out of his skin and the other brownies giggled very small giggles with their hands over their mouths.

Old Grandfather came in and sat down in HIS chair. He sighed too.

"Well, my dear," he said, "this old house makes a lot of work for us."

"Too much work for OUR old bones," agreed Old Grandmother.

"Perhaps we should look at that LABORSAVING house we heard about. There is no harm in that, is there?" Old Grandfather asked.

"Well, no-o-o," said Old Grandmother. "I like this old house, but I think you should take a look at the new one. You can tell me all about it. If you think it is EXACTLY the right house for us, you may decide."

"I'll go now," said Old Grandfather, and he went out and climbed into his old jalopy.

So most of the brownies went to play in the pine woods. But Biggest Brownie, Middle-Size Brownie and

Smallest Brownie hid near the little white house watching to see Old Grandfather come back.

At last he came, looking rather pleased with himself. Biggest Brownie rushed off to tell the other brownies to come quickly, while Middle-Size Brownie crept into the house behind Old Grandfather.

In no time at all ALL the brownies were hiding under Old Grandmother's chair, listening.

"Tell me all about it," said Old Grandmother eagerly. "Is it LABORSAVING?"

"It's LABORSAVING and lovely," Old Grandfather said. "It is white with green shutters, and it looks a little like our old house, but it's NEW. I did what you said: I decided."

"You decided we should have it?" Old Grandmother asked, her eyes shining.

"Yes, it is ours," said Old Grandfather.

THEN Old Grandmother looked a little anxious. "How shall we ever manage to pack all our belongings?" she asked. "Our old bones will be too stiff and tired."

"All the same it has to be done. We'll manage somehow," said Old Grandfather. Then to make Old Grandmother happy again he said, "The little white house is in an apple orchard—AND I saw a bluebird fly by. It looks at a mountain too."

"A house in an orchard AND a mountain to look at!" exclaimed Old Grandmother. "I've always wanted a house that looks at a mountain. I only hope our old bones will last through all that packing. If I had one big wish, I'd wish those brownies would help us."

The brownies almost exploded and made merry

little signs to one another that they certainly would help all they could.

"Well, Old Grandfather," said Old Grandmother, "you must be tired after that big journey. Let's take our old bones upstairs for an afternoon nap. Then we can do a little packing afterwards."

The brownies heard Old Grandmother and Old Grandfather go STUMP-STUMP-STUMP up the stairs and scurried out from under the chair.

"What shall we do?" asked Middle-Size Brownie.

"What shall we do?" echoed Smallest Brownie, jiggling on his toes excitedly.

"First, we'll hunt around for little boxes and little things to pack, just the right size for brownies," Biggest Brownie said.

So the brownies scurried around, looking in every

nook and cranny for boxes just the right size. They found quite a collection. Two or three brownies had to carry some boxes that were rather big.

"Hurry, brownies, before Old Grandmother and Old Grandfather come downstairs. We have some boxes, now we must pack," said Biggest Brownie.

The brownies were busy as could be. Some brought spoons, some forks—and eggcups, and peppers and salts.

Only the biggest, most CAREFUL brownies could carry the knives, and two had to carry each knife.

Middle-Size Brownie and two or three other brownies wrapped some of the cups and saucers in tissue paper VERY carefully.

But Smallest Brownie was full of curiosity. He was poking into this and looking into that, when the other brownies were too busy to watch him.

Suddenly, a small voice was heard crying, "Help! Help!" But it did not sound like Smallest Brownie's voice. It was a voice that sounded HOLLOW.

All the brownies stopped working and listened.

Biggest Brownie and Middle-Size Brownie began
to look around for Smallest Brownie, and all the time
the small HOLLOW voice was calling, "Help! Help!"

"That must be Smallest Brownie," said Biggest Brownie.

"It's a very QUEER voice," Middle-Size Brownie said. "What makes Smallest Brownie's voice so HOLLOW?"

"Maybe he has fallen inside a cup," Biggest Brownie suggested, "a cup with a round HOLLOW sound."

They looked in this cup and that. But Smallest Brownie was not in any cup.

As they looked here and there they came near Old Grandmother's teapot. They almost jumped out of their skins, because the small HOLLOW voice called loudly, "Help! Help! I'm inside the TEAPOT."

"How did you get in there?" asked Middle-Size

Brownie, clambering up the handle and peering over

the rim at Smallest Brownie who was in a sad little heap at the bottom.

"I climbed up the handle to look inside," Smallest Brownie replied in a very small voice. "I slipped and fell in."

By now Biggest Brownie was sitting astraddle on the teapot handle behind Middle-Size Brownie. "You reach down and grab Smallest Brownie's hands, while I hold onto your feet, so that YOU will not fall in too," he said.

So Middle-Size Brownie reached DOWN as far as he could, and Smallest Brownie reached UP as far as he could and Biggest Brownie held on tight to Middle-Size Brownie's feet.

With a heave and a pull, and a heave and a pull, up came Smallest Brownie. They all fell in a heap as they slid off the handle.

"We had better find something useful for Smallest Brownie to do," said Biggest Brownie and he gave Smallest Brownie a crayon he had found. "Smallest Brownie," he said, "you draw pictures on the lids of boxes telling what is inside."

Smallest Brownie was very happy. He had a lovely time making pictures of cups and spoons and salts and peppers.

Of course, when they woke up, Old Grandmother and Old Grandfather were DELIGHTED to find that the brownies had been around to help.

Every day the old people worked and every day when Old Grandmother and Old Grandfather were resting, the brownies came creepity-creep, creepity-creep to help.

Just before a big moving van came to take every-

thing away to the new house, three brownies packed Old Grandmother's precious teapot. They were VERY, VERY careful. Smallest Brownie made a picture on the box.

The big van pulled up to the door, everything was packed inside and Old Grandmother and Old Grandfather went ahead in their old jalopy.

"Goodness!" shrieked Biggest Brownie. "We must go in the van to help UNpack."

"Yes, yes, quick, quick, climb up," Middle-Size
Brownie called.

So the brownies climbed up a rope that was dangling at the back of the van, just as it moved off.

Middle-Size Brownie made sure Smallest Brownie climbed up too.

The little white house and the pine woods were soon out of sight and, as the van jogged along, Smallest Brownie said in a wobbly voice, "HOW ARE WE GOING TO GET HOME AGAIN?"

THAT made all the brownies think. Biggest Brownie thought a long time. Then he made up his mind and said in a big firm voice, "WE'RE moving too."

"WE are moving?" asked the other brownies, very much surprised.

"Yes," said Biggest Brownie, "there will be apple trees and roots in the orchard. Maybe we'll find LABORSAVING homes for ourselves."

When at last they reached the new house, Old Grandmother and Old Grandfather were at the door waiting. The apple trees had pink flowers, bees buzzed

around them, the sky was blue, a bluebird flew by and the mountain was grand and serene.

"It's BEAUTIFUL," said all the brownies, "really and truly BEAUTIFUL."

Then began such an UNpacking. While the old people were in one room the brownies were in another. They looked inside closets, they pranced on the new floors, they patted pillows and sat on the chairs left by the moving men.

At last the old people were out of the kitchen and the brownies were there by themselves.

They tried to turn on the bright new faucets.
They slid on the new stainless steel sink and pretended
to skate on the shiny new counters.

Then Smallest Brownie saw the box with the picture of Old Grandmother's teapot on the lid. "Look!" he said, pointing. "Look! There's my teapot."

"Old Grandmother's teapot!" exclaimed Middle-Size Brownie. "Old Grandmother will be wanting her cup of tea. Let's unpack it."

Biggest Brownie and Middle-Size Brownie, helped

by Smallest Brownie, took the teapot out of the box very CAREFULLY and put it on the shiny new counter. Some of the other brownies unpacked two cups and two saucers and put them beside the teapot.

Smallest Brownie found the tea and put it there too. He was very pleased with himself. Then they all hid behind a big carton.

Old Grandfather came into the kitchen. "Old Grandmother needs a cup of tea," he was saying to himself. "Now, where's her precious teapot?"

When he saw it and the tea, the cups and saucers

on the counter, he could hardly believe his eyes. He

hurried to where Old Grandmother was sitting in her chair, surrounded by furniture.

"The brownies must have come with us," he said. "Come and see."

Old Grandmother pulled her tired old bones from her chair. When she saw everything ready for tea, she said, "Bless their little hearts! They must have moved with us."

The brownies were DELIGHTED. They hugged themselves with joy and smiled their wide smiles.

When Old Grandmother and Old Grandfather had finished their tea, they went out to look at the orchard. "We must see whether there are good homes for brownies under the apple-tree roots," Old Grandmother said.

"Yes," said Old Grandfather, "there are lots of places brownies could find to live in. I'll make little tables and stools just the right size for brownies' homes."

"And I'll make things for them too," Old Grandmother said.

The old people went back to their new home and the brownies went to find new homes for themselves. They looked at this old gnarled root and at that one.

There were lots of places for brownie homes, just as Old Grandfather had said.

They did not really know what LABORSAVING meant, but Biggest Brownie said, "There are plenty of LABORSAVING homes here—we can have apples without any trouble at all."

They settled happily into their new homes and every day brought new surprises. One day there were

tables and little stools outside their homes, another day
there were lace tablecloths, and acorn cup bowls too—

and there was a clothesline strung between posts. The brownies danced with glee.

Every day they crept into the new white house with the green shutters to help the old people and every day the two old people had a new surprise for the brownies. Sometimes it was milk in their little bowls, sometimes tiny cakes just the right size for brownies.

So EVERYONE was contented.

EVERYONE was happy.